Mallory vs Max

To my parents, who perfected the art of loving
individually, and to my sisters, who made growing up fun!
With all my heart,
LBF

Laurie - you stole my dedication!
To MY parents, who astoundingly raised six!
Thanks for always providing me with an art studio.
Love,
T

by Laurie Friedman
illustrations by Tamara Schmitz

Lerner Books • London • New York • Minneapolis

CONTENTS

A WORD FROM MALLORY

Fact: You don't get to choose your brother or your bedtime.

I know. I'm Mallory McDonald, age 8 ¾ plus 1 month, and I got stuck with a brother and a bedtime I never would have chosen myself.

First, let me tell you about my bedtime. It's 8.30. My brother Max, who is 10, gets to stay up until 9.30.

A later bedtime isn't all Max gets. He's getting a dog!

You're probably thinking that's good news, that dogs are cute and fun. Even though I'm a cat person, I don't disagree. The thing is, ever since Mum and Dad said Max could get a dog, that's all anyone in this house ever talks about.

Take last night at dinner, for example. When I told Mum I needed new trainers, she said we should wait, that we wouldn't want the dog to chew up a new pair of shoes. She and Dad and Max laughed, but not me. It made my toes hurt just thinking about it.

So this morning, I tried talking to my parents. 'I don't know why we're getting a dog. We already have a cat — Cheeseburger. Remember her?'

I don't think my parents remembered my cat or me because right in the middle of my talk, Max barged in with a book about dogs and faster than you can say flea powder, my parents were talking to Max as if I wasn't even in the room.

Fact: Ever since my parents said Max could get a dog, things in this house haven't been so good for me.

Another fact: Once we actually get the dog, I'm scared they're going to get a whole lot worse.

MALLORY MARCHES

I started a new club.

It's called SABGD. That's short for Sisters Against Brothers Getting Dogs.

Right now, I'm the president and the only member of the club, but soon things will change. When other girls see how much attention their brothers get when their parents say, *'You can get a dog,'* they will want to join my club too.

I will teach club members to protest.

I will teach club members to speak out.

I will teach club members to march, which is what I'm doing right now.

I march into the kitchen with my cat, Cheeseburger and pass out flyers to Mum and Dad. 'Mallory McDonald, founding member of Sisters Against Brothers Getting Dogs, has something to say,' I shout through my megaphone.

Mum and Dad put down their coffee cups and stare at me.

I put down my megaphone and start reading.

10 Reasons Why I, Mallory McDonald, Think Max should NOT get a dog.

Reason 1: Dogs eat a lot. Not only dog food... shoes too!

Reason 2: Dogs drink a lot. They drink out of toilets. If you kiss Max's dog, it will be the same thing as drinking out of a toilet.

Reason 3: Dogs dig a lot. Max's dog will dig in our garden and in our neighbours' gardens. No one on our street will like us if Max gets a dog.

Reason 4: Dogs bark a lot. If Max gets a dog, it will bark all night and we will never get a good night's sleep.

Reason 5: Dogs poop a lot. In the winter, our back garden will look like a giant chocolate chip cookie.

Reason 6: Dogs chase away important people, like binmen and paper boys.

Reason 7: Dogs need a lot of attention. They want everybody to look at them and pet them and say how cute they are... all of the time!

Reason 8: Dogs make people say stupid things. Max will start saying stupid things like, 'The dog ate my homework.'

Reason 9: Dogs have to be taken care of. MAX WILL NOT DO THIS! You will be the one taking care of the dog!

Reason 10: We already have a pet—CHEESEBURGER! Her feelings will be very, very, very hurt if we get another pet!

I finish reading my flyer and wait. I'm waiting for Mum and Dad to say, *'Mallory, that makes sense. You're right. We're wrong. We won't get a dog for Max.'*

That's not what they say though. Dad tells me to sit down. 'Mallory, I'm not sure I understand why you're so upset about Max getting a dog,' he says.

'Lots of reasons,' I tell Dad. 'I just gave you ten of them.'

Dad reads from the list. 'I'm not worried about the eating, drinking, digging, barking and pooing. That's what dogs do.'

'What about number six?' I ask Dad. 'What about chasing away binmen and paper boys? What are you going to do when we have rubbish piled up to the roof, and you don't know what's going on in the world?'

Dad smiles. 'That's a good point. We'll

keep the dog inside when the binmen and the paper boy show up.'

'What about seven? Your hand will get tired from petting a dog *all* the time.'

Dad laughs.

I wave my list in his face. 'How about eight? Aren't you worried that Max won't do his homework because he'll be too busy playing with a dog?'

Dad shakes his head.

I point my finger at reason number nine. 'If we get a dog, Max won't take care of it. You and Mum will have to do all the work. Did you think about that?' I ask Dad.

Dad nods. 'Max knows he's responsible for taking care of this dog.'

'Well, what about ten? Aren't you worried about Cheeseburger?'

Dad looks me straight in the eye. 'I'm not worried about one, two, three, four,

five, six, seven, eight or even nine, but yes, ten concerns me.'

Finally, Dad is starting to see my point, and it's about time.

I cover Cheeseburger's ears. 'Ten should concern you. How do you think Cheeseburger will feel if we get a dog?'

'Cheeseburger isn't the one I'm worried about,' says Dad. 'It might take some time, but Cheeseburger will get used to a new dog.' Dad smiles at me. 'Sweet Potato, getting a dog will be fun.'

Getting a dog will be fun for *some* people, but not *all* people. I cross my arms. 'Getting a dog will be fun for Max,' I tell Dad.

Mum gives Dad an *I'll-take-it-from-here* look. 'Mallory, you need to change your attitude. Getting a dog will be fun for our whole family. Dogs are so lovable, and whatever dog we get will love everybody in our family,' Mum says.

I pick up a flyer and wave it at Mum and Dad. 'Didn't you read this?'

'I'd like to read it if you don't mind,' says a voice behind me.

Max plucks my flyer out of my hand. He reads it, then crushes it into a ball and tosses it in the bin. 'I *won't* say the dog ate my homework, and I *will* take care of it!'

Mum pours herself some more coffee. 'Let's all calm down,' she says.

'Mum, Dad,' says Max. 'I promised I

would take care of this dog, and I will. Mallory has a cat. I'm getting a dog. Fair is fair.'

'I didn't *get* a cat,' I remind Max. 'I found a cat and I got to keep her.'

Max must be the only brother on the planet who doesn't understand the difference between rescuing an abandoned animal and getting a pet when you already have one.

Max shrugs. 'If you ask me, it doesn't matter how you got your pet. It just matters that you have one, and now, I'll have one too. Right, Dad?'

'I think we'll all enjoy having a dog,' says Dad. He puts his coffee cup in the sink. Then he looks at me. 'We're getting a dog and that's final. We'll start our search at the pet shop on Saturday.'

Dad picks up his car keys. 'See you all later. I have to go to work.'

I wait until I hear his car pull out of the driveway. Then I pick up my megaphone. 'Not fair! Not fair! Not fair!' I shout through the little opening.

Max looks at me as if I'm a dirt stain on his baseball shirt. Then he makes rings around his ear with his finger like I'm crazy. 'What a weirdo.'

I ignore Max. Thoughts of other girls who, one day, might have to go through what I'm going through fill my brain.

I pick up Cheeseburger and march across the kitchen. 'Sisters Against Brothers Getting Dogs!' I shout through my megaphone.

'Mallory, that's enough,' says Mum.

'This march has just begun,' I tell her.

I march around the kitchen table and

into the dining room. 'SISTERS AGAINST BROTHERS GETTING DOGS!' I chant.

When I march back into the kitchen, my march is stopped by a blockade . . . a mum blockade.

Mum takes my megaphone and holds it up to her mouth. 'There's only one place you need to march, young lady, and that's straight to your room!'

LIFE'S NOT FAIR!

'No peeping!' I pull Mum and Dad by their hands and sit them down on my bed. I've been waiting all week for Saturday to get here and now that it's here, I don't want to spoil the surprise. 'OK,' I say. 'Open your eyes!'

When my parents open their eyes, they look very surprised.

'Mallory, why are all your scrapbooks on the floor of your room instead of on the shelf in your wardrobe?' Mum asks me.

'It's Scrapbook Day!' I tell her. I put Cheeseburger in Mum's lap and pick up a pink scrapbook with the word Kindergarten on the cover. 'You and Dad and I are going to spend the day looking at all of my old scrapbooks.'

Dad raises an eyebrow. 'Mallory, today we're going to . . . '

Before Dad can finish his sentence, I plop down on the bed between Mum and Dad and open my Kindergarten scrapbook to a picture of me with a big bow in my hair and a little backpack on wheels. 'This is me on my first day of school.'

Mum looks over my shoulder at Dad.

I start turning pages. I show them a picture of me eating a snack at break time and a picture of me pushing a shopping trolley on a class day out to the supermarket.

Dad clears his throat. 'Mallory . . .'

I close my Kindergarten scrapbook.
'Now we're going to look at my First Grade
scrapbook.' I reach for a thick, blue book
with alphabet letters on it, but when I do, a
pair of black trainers are blocking my way.
'Move it,' I tell Max, but he doesn't.

'Dad, when are we going to the pet
shop?' asks Max. 'It's Saturday and you
said we could look for a dog today.'

I reach around Max's leg to get my First
Grade scrapbook. 'Mum and Dad can't go
today. It's Scrapbook Day.'

'Scrapbook Day?' Max laughs. 'We're going to the pet shop. Right, Dad?'

I ignore Max, open my scrapbook and point to a picture of me carrying a lunch box. 'Dad, isn't this a cute picture?'

Dad isn't looking at the picture though. He looks at Mum. Then he looks at me.

'Mallory, I love looking at all these pictures of you, but we had planned to go to the pet shop today. What do you say we do Scrapbook Day tomorrow?'

I turn the page. 'Here I am writing on the blackboard.'

Dad puts his arm around me. 'Sweet Potato, you need to put the scrapbooks away. We're going to the pet shop.'

I cross my arms. 'You and Mum and Max planned to go to the pet shop, but nobody asked me if that's what I wanted to do.'

'I'm sure we'll all have fun,' says Mum.

She puts Cheeseburger on my bed and starts picking up scrapbooks. 'We'll help you clean up and then we'll go.'

'Great,' says Max. He grabs a scrapbook and throws it into my wardrobe.

It lands on a pile of shoes. 'Mum! Tell Max to be careful with my stuff.'

'Max!' Mum gives Max a stern look.

Max shrugs his shoulders and gives Mum a *what-did-I-do-wrong* look, but I know he knows what he did wrong.

'I'll finish here,' says Mum. 'Why don't you two go outside for a few minutes.'

'Is it OK if I go next door and see if Joey wants to come to the pet shop with us?' Max asks Dad. 'Since he has a dog, he could be a big help.'

'I think that's a fine idea,' says Dad. 'Why don't you and Mallory go together.'

Max walks towards the front door.

I scoop up Cheeseburger and follow Max outside. I have to run-walk to keep up with him. Joey is my friend, not Max's! Max even says that living next door to Joey is the worst part of living on Wish Pond Road.

Just because Max is getting a dog and Joey has one doesn't mean Max can steal my friends. 'Since when do you care what Joey thinks?' I ask Max.

Max pushes the Winstons' doorbell. 'Joey is a dog expert.'

'That's not fair!' I say to Max. 'You can't just take my friends.'

'Life's not fair,' says Max as if he's an old, smart person talking to a young, stupid one. Then he starts laughing.

When Joey opens the front door, Max stops laughing and starts explaining. 'The thing is, I don't know what kind of dog I want to get. Want to help me pick?'

Joey smiles. 'OK! But you'll know the right dog when you see it.' Joey pats his dog, Murphy. 'I knew the minute I saw Murphy that he was for me.'

Max nods his head like that makes sense to him, like it's something that only a kid getting a dog could understand.

'Come in,' says Joey. 'Let me put on my sweatshirt and we'll go.' Max follows Joey down the hall. I go into the Winstons' kitchen. Winnie is at the table peeling an orange.

'What do you want?' she says without looking up.

'Max is getting a dog. He came over to see if Joey would go to the pet shop with us. Want to come too?' I ask.

Winnie pops a piece of orange into her mouth and chews it slowly. 'I wouldn't go to a pet shop if it were the last place on the planet,' she says when she stops chewing.

I sit down at the table holding Cheeseburger. Now that Max is getting a dog, Winnie and I have a lot in common. 'So what's it like having a brother with a dog?'

Winnie makes a face like she's about to get a shot. 'Get ready.'

'For what?'

Winnie raises an eyebrow. 'When Joey got Murphy, everybody treated that dog like he was the president.'

I think about all the attention Max *already* gets and he hasn't even got a dog yet. 'It must have been pretty bad,' I say to Winnie.

Winnie laughs. 'That wasn't the worst part. The worst part is *having* a dog. Soon you'll step in things that make a used lump of gum seem like a birthday present. And your clothes will be covered in dog hairs.'

She picks one off her shirt and hands it to me.

'It's awful,' continues Winnie. 'I refuse to even say the word *D-O-G*. If you think your life is bad now, just wait.'

I pick up Cheeseburger. 'Thanks,' I say. 'I have to be going.'

'Watch where you step,' she says as I'm leaving.

When I get home, I go into my room, shut the door and pull out my

Cheeseburger scrapbook. I snuggle up on my bed with her. 'Want to see your baby book?' I ask her.

I open the first page and tell Cheeseburger the story of how I found her.

'Once upon a time, there was a teeny, tiny kitten that lost her mother. The kitten wandered into the garden of a little girl.'

I show Cheeseburger a picture of me holding her when she was a baby.

'The little girl put out a bowl of milk and some food. She thought the kitten would leave and go to look for her mother, but the kitten stayed. So the little girl took the kitten inside and made a bed for her on her pillow.'

I show Cheeseburger a picture of her sleeping on top of my bed in my old house.

'The little girl thought the kitten was happy there. But just to be sure, she went

next door to get her lifelong best friend, who agreed that the kitten must love her a lot. Together, they convinced the little girl's mother to let her keep the kitten.'

I show Cheeseburger a picture of Mary Ann and me holding her.

'The little girl named her kitten Cheeseburger after her favourite food and they lived happily ever after . . . until the little girl grew up, moved to a new town, left behind her old best friend and then tragically learned that her older brother was going to get a dog.'

I close Cheeseburger's baby book and rub her back. 'Max is right about one thing,' I tell her. 'Life's not fair.'

KING MAX

'Welcome to the Pet Palace!' A lady carrying a sceptre and wearing a crown with the name *Patsy* on it greets us at the door. 'What can I do for you?'

Dad puts his arm around Max. 'This young man is looking for a dog.'

Patsy picks up a paper crown and a brightly coloured pen. 'What's this young man's name?'

When Dad introduces Max, Patsy writes *Max* on the front of the paper crown and plops it on Max's head. 'At the Pet Palace, pets rule, and so do our customers.'

Patsy points her sceptre to the back of the shop. 'To the dog kingdom!'

If you ask me, Max is too old to wear a crown and too young to be a king, but I follow them to the dog kingdom.

Max grins at Joey as we pass through the fish kingdom and the bird kingdom. 'I can't wait to get a dog,' he says to Joey.

'Yeah,' says Joey. 'We're going to have so much fun playing with our dogs.'

Just thinking about Max and

Joey playing with their dogs does sound like fun . . . *fun that doesn't include me.* A week ago, Max and Joey barely spoke to each other and now they're practically best friends.

Mum said we would *all* have fun at the pet shop, but so far, I'm not having such a good time. When we pass through the cat kingdom, I stop and pick up a box of cat claw polish. I tug on Mum's sleeve. 'Mum, can I please get this? Please!'

I read Mum the little poem on the side of the box:

A colour for each day of the week
So your cat will have lovely claws.
With Colour Me Happy Polish Kit,
Your cat will have mighty fine paws!

Mum looks at the box in my hands.

'Mallory, we bought a new collar for Cheeseburger last week. Today we're here to look at dogs.' She puts the polish back on the shelf. 'We can get polish another day.' Mum walks towards the dog kingdom.

I follow her. I know I'm not getting polish today. Here's what else I'm not getting: How come Max is getting *everything* he wants and I'm not getting *anything* I want?

I start to tap Mum on the shoulder so I can explain how she could make this trip to the pet shop fun for *everybody,* but Patsy taps me on the shoulder with her sceptre.

'Over here,' she says. Patsy opens a cage filled with furry puppies, takes one out and hands it to Max. 'For you, King Max.'

Max rolls the puppy around in his hands. I didn't want Max to get a dog, but the one he's holding is so little and cute, I could see myself liking her. I could even see Cheeseburger liking her. Maybe they could become best friends, like Mary Ann and me. Maybe getting a dog won't be so bad.

I walk over to Max and rub the puppy's back. 'We should get this dog,' I say to him. 'She's so little and cute.'

'I don't want a little, cute dog. I want a

big dog.' Max hands the puppy back to Patsy. I watch while she puts the dog back into the cage.

'I think that dog would make a great pet,' I say to Max.

'Maybe you think that dog would make a great pet, but I don't.' Max pushes his crown on top of his head. 'And this is going to be my dog.'

I think Max is taking this king stuff far too seriously.

'Mum said this dog will love everybody in our family. So everybody in our family ought to get to help decide what kind of dog we get.'

Max ignores me and keeps looking inside cages.

'How about this dog?' I say, pointing to a white, fluffy dog.

Max looks at the white, fluffy dog. 'I don't want a white, fluffy dog.' Max walks up and down the rows of cages filled with dogs. He stops in front of each one, then shakes his head like none of the dogs are quite right.

'Mum, Dad,' says Max. 'I just don't see a dog here that I want.'

'Remember what I told you,' says Joey. 'You'll know the right dog when you see it.'

I give Mum and Dad a *parents-not-Joey-are-supposed-to-know-best* look. 'Mum, Dad, you know how you always make us try new foods? You tell us we won't know what we like unless we try it. I think it's the same thing with dogs.'

I point to the white fluffy dog. 'Max won't know if he likes this dog unless he tries it.'

Max rolls his eyes, like that's the dumbest thing he's ever heard. 'Joey said I would know when I see the right dog and I don't.'

Dad puts his arm around Max. 'What else can you show us?' he asks Patsy.

Patsy walks around the dog kingdom looking inside the cages. 'At the Pet Palace, we pride ourselves on having something for everyone, but I don't think we have what your son is looking for,' Patsy tells Dad.

Max hangs his head. His crown falls off.

Patsy picks it up and pushes it back down on top of his hair. 'How about a pet pig? If you feed them right, they get huge. I had one that got so big, it won a blue ribbon at the state fair.'

Max looks disappointed. In a way, I feel sorry for him. I know how sad I would be if I didn't have Cheeseburger.

Suddenly, Patsy's eyes light up. 'I've got it!' She points her scepter to the cat kingdom. 'How about a kitten? You can even pretend it's a dog and soon you'll love it so much, you'll forget you ever wanted a dog.'

'That's a great idea!' I say. 'Patsy doesn't have a dog you want, so get a cat. Cheeseburger will have a playmate.'

Max looks at me like I asked him to stick his head in the toilet. 'I'm not getting a cat. Cats are boring. I want a dog.'

'Cats aren't boring.' Dad looks in Max's direction. 'But we did come here to get a dog. Maybe we'd better do a little more looking,' he says to Patsy.

Dad is right. We should do a little more looking . . . for a new brother!

Max didn't even consider the kind of dog I wanted to get! He said cats are boring! I'm glad Cheeseburger wasn't here to hear this. I'm sorry I ever felt sorry for Max!

Patsy sighs. 'I wish I had something for you. We like to keep our customers happy.' Then she waves her sceptre like she's casting a magic spell. 'I'll tell you what. I have a friend who has a farm a few hours north of here. He has a litter of puppies that he's trying to find nice homes for. Why don't I give you his phone number.'

Dad nods. 'That would be great.'

Patsy writes the phone number down on a piece of paper and hands it to Dad. 'Give him a call and see if you can take a ride up there tomorrow. Maybe those puppies will be more like what you had in mind.'

Dad folds the slip of paper Patsy gave him and puts it in his pocket. 'Thanks for your help,' says Dad.

Patsy tips her crown. 'When it comes to pets, Patsy knows best. Now, hurry back to the Pet Palace. Once you get your pet, we've got everything you'll need to make his home seem like a kingdom.'

Then she smiles at us. 'Good luck, King Max. I have a good feeling about this.'

Max grins. 'Me too.'

'Me three,' says Dad.

'Me four,' says Mum.

'Me five,' says Joey.

Everybody looks at me. 'Me six,' I mumble. The only feeling I have is that I liked Max better before he was crowned king.

MAX'S DAY

'Welcome to Skyline Farm.' Farmer Frank shakes Dad's hand as we get out of the car. He looks at Max. 'You must be the young man looking for a dog.'

Max nods his head.

'Excellent!' Farmer Frank slaps Max on the back. 'I bet you're in a hurry to see the cute little creatures.'

Maybe Max is in a hurry to see the cute little creatures, but I'm in a hurry to see my best friend. I tug on Mum's sleeve. 'When will Mary Ann be here?'

Mum looks at her watch and smiles. 'Mary Ann's house is about an hour from here. Her mum said they would get here as early as possible.'

I still can't believe Mum called Mary Ann's mum. I think back to last night.

I went into Mum and Dad's room and explained to them that ever since they said Max could get a dog, I haven't felt like a very important part of this family.

Dad said I am a super important part of this family and Mum said she had a super idea. That's when she called Mary Ann's mum to see if they would meet us here today. Mum said she knew today would be special for Max and she wanted it to be special for me too.

Having Mary Ann here will make today extra special for me!

I throw my arms around Mum and hug her. 'Thanks again for inviting Mary Ann to meet us.' Mum kisses my forehead, then points down the dirt track that leads to the farm. 'Look who I see.'

A blue car is coming our way. 'It's Mary Ann!' I shout.

'Great,' mumbles Max. 'I can't wait to see Birdbrain.'

I know Max isn't excited to see my lifelong best friend, but I am. Ever since we moved to Fern Falls, I hardly ever get to see Mary Ann.

Mary Ann's mum pulls her car to a stop in front of us and Mary Ann hops out.

'We're here! We're here! We're here! I thought we'd never get here!' She hugs me. Then she looks around as if she's looking for something and she can't find it.

'Where are the puppies?' Mary Ann asks.

'Right this way.' Farmer Frank motions us to follow him through a barn.

I follow Farmer Frank, but I can't believe Mary Ann. She hasn't seen me for exactly one month, two weeks, four days and six hours, and she hardly even said hello. My own best friend is more interested in a puppy she doesn't even know than in me.

I pull on Mary Ann's elbow. 'Puppies can be pretty boring,' I whisper in her ear.

Then I hold my nose. 'And kind of stinky too. Let's go play while Max picks one.'

I wait for Mary Ann to say, *'OK! Let's go and play! That sounds like a lot more fun than looking at boring, stinky puppies.'* That's not what she says though.

'Look!' Mary Ann points to a small pen behind the barn.

'Say hello to the puppies,' says Farmer Frank.

He unlatches the gate to the pen. 'The puppies are only eight weeks old. They're still little, so you have to handle 'em carefully.'

'C'mon.' I tug on Mary Ann's sleeve. Mary Ann doesn't move. She has a look on her face that people get in cartoons when they're falling in love, and Mary Ann isn't the only one with that look on her face.

Mum, Dad, Max, Joey, even Mary Ann's mum have it too. They're all staring at the puppies as if they've been bitten by a love bug.

'C'mon in.' Farmer Frank gestures to us to follow him.

Dad motions for Max to go first.

When Max walks into the pen, the puppies scamper to his feet. Max rubs their backs. 'Wow, they're so cute. It's going to be hard to choose one.'

'Pick 'em up and see which one you fancy,' Farmer Frank says to Max.

Max starts picking up puppies. He picks up a brown one, then a black one, then a white one and then a brown one with a white patch of fur around one eye. Max looks from puppy to puppy. 'This might take a while.'

'It's a big decision,' says Dad. 'Take your time.'

'C'mon.' I try to pull Mary Ann away from the puppies. 'Let's go look around the farm.'

'Let's stay here,' says Mary Ann. 'Picking a puppy is a lot more exciting than looking around a farm.' Mary Ann starts jumping up and down again. 'I can't wait to see which puppy Max picks.'

I look at the puppy Max is holding. I try to guess which one he's going to pick. I know which one I would pick, but I know it won't be the same one Max will pick. Even though we're brother and sister, we never seem to like the same things.

Mum points to the little brown puppy with the white patch of fur around his eye. He's licking Max's hand. 'Look Max, I think that puppy likes you.'

Max rubs his back.

Joey smiles. 'He likes you a lot.'

I know Mum said this puppy would love everybody in our family, but if it's Max's dog, I wonder if it will love me too.

While Max is deciding which puppy to pick, I do what I always do when I want something to happen and I'm not sure it's going to. I pretend like I'm at the wish pond on my road and have found a wish pebble. I make a wish. *I wish Max will pick a puppy that will like me too.* I pretend to throw my wish pebble in the wish pond so my wish will come true.

'Hey,' says Max. 'This puppy really does like me.' The brown puppy is licking Max's face.

Max hugs the puppy. 'I know this is the puppy for me.'

Joey grins. 'I told you you'd know when you found the right one.'

'That's a good choice,' says Farmer

Frank. 'That puppy is the smartest and fastest of all the puppies. I've seen a lot of dogs and that one's a real champ.'

Farmer Frank pulls a sheet of paper out of his back pocket and hands it to Max.

'Here are some instructions on how to take care of your new dog. Just remember: love your dog, feed your dog, walk your dog and be consistent. Dogs like routine.'

'Don't worry, I'll take really good care of him,' says Max.

'I'm sure you will,' says Farmer Frank. He and Dad talk for a few minutes. Then Farmer Frank waves goodbye.

Everyone crowds around Max and his new puppy. Mum starts taking pictures.

Mary Ann's mum rubs the puppy's back. 'What are you going to call him?'

Mary Ann tickles the puppy's tummy.

'Does he get to sleep in your room?'

Joey scratches behind the puppy's ears. 'Do you want me to help you train him?'

Mary Ann kisses the puppy on his nose. 'Oh, he's so, so, so cute! You're so, so, so lucky you're getting a puppy,' Mary Ann says to me as if I'm the one getting the puppy.

This is Max's puppy though, not mine. I feel as if today was extra special for Max, but I don't feel it was extra special for me. Even having my best friend here didn't help.

Dad smiles at the puppy in Max's arms like it's a new baby. 'We can go back to the pet shop later and get everything he needs.'

'I can't wait to take him home,' says Max.

Home. I think about Max taking his

new puppy home. I don't know what home will be like with Max's new puppy, but one thing's for sure – life at 17 Wish Pond Road will never be the same.

IN THE DOGHOUSE

I slam my door. Then I open it and slam it again . . . harder this time. I'm waiting for someone to say, *'Mallory, stop slamming your door.'* But no one says a word.

I open my bedroom door and slam it shut as hard as I can. I really don't think that shouting at a dog for chewing up my favourite fuzzy duck slippers and knocking over my Purple Passion nail polish is, as

Mum says, *'out of line.'*

I am mad. I am misunderstood. I am stuck in my room for what Mum calls *'unacceptable behaviour.'*

Even though I'm not too happy that Mary Ann practically ignored me on the farm, I do the only thing any girl in my position could do. I take out a sheet of paper and start a letter to my best friend.

Dear Mary Ann,

Do you know what it means when someone says you're in the doghouse?

It means you're in big, big, big trouble. Right now, Mum says I'm in the doghouse. If you ask me, Mum is right. I AM in the doghouse . . . I LIVE in a doghouse!

It has been exactly five days since Max got his dog and all anyone in this house talks about anymore is max's dog!

Max's dog is so cute. Max's dog is so sweet. Max's dog is so smart.

max's dog! max's dog! max's dog! max's dog doesn't even have a name yet. (He will probably grow up thinking his name is 'max's dog.')

When people are not talking about max's dog, they are playing with him or petting him or walking him or buying things for him or teaching him how not to poo on the carpet.

I'm starting to think the only way to get any attention around here is to poo on the carpet. (Don't worry. I'm not going to try it!)

So this morning, I told Mum we needed to have a little talk.

I told her that Max and his dog are getting ALL the attention and that it is really starting to bother me and Cheeseburger too and that both of us are starting to feel like poor, unwanted animals.

Do you know what she told me?

She told me that a new puppy requires a lot of attention and that she thinks I haven't been doing my part to make the dog feel welcome and that it is really starting to bother her and Dad too and that both of them are starting to feel that if I don't change my attitude soon, I'm going to be punished.

CAN YOU BELIEVE IT?

So I told Mum that I tried to have a good attitude but that I feel like everybody in this house has forgotten that my cat and I even live here. I told her I just don't understand why we had to go and get a dog when we already had a perfectly good cat.

So mum said she was giving me something I could understand. She sent me to my room to think about my behaviour. She even sent Cheeseburger, who she says 'doesn't seem too keen on the dog yet.'

(If you're wondering what that means, see drawing at bottom of letter.)

mum said that when I come out, she wants to see a brand-new attitude.

She forgot to say, 'IF I come out.' She should have said that, because I am planning to stay in my room with Cheeseburger forever, which is why I am writing to you. Can you please send us a few things?

Food: chocolate doughnuts (a lifetime supply), cheese pizza, marshmallows, make-your-own-sundae supplies (don't forget sprinkles) and cat food

Clothes: T-shirts, pyjama bottoms, new slippers (the fuzzy duck kind, size 3) and a new pair of sunglasses (see if you can find the purple, sparkly ones)

Supplies: stickers, glue, paper, pens, nail polish (send lots, I am completely out), and hair thingies

When you send the package, send it to my address, in care of:

Mallory McDonald (who will be in her room for the rest of her life).

Thank you! Thank you! Thank you!

You are the best friend a girl could ever, ever, ever have!

Hugs and kisses,
   mallory

PS THE CRUEL AND UNFAIR
TREATMENT OF CHEESEBURGER
written and illustrated by mallory mcDonald

PLAYING GAMES

QUESTION: How do you get a girl to change her attitude and come out of her room when she's 100% convinced she's never, ever, ever going to?

ANSWER: Order a pizza.

I wasn't going to change my attitude or come out of my room, but then I smelled pizza.

'What's going on?' I ask as I walk into the kitchen. Max and his dog and Joey are at the table. When I sit down holding

Cheeseburger, Max's dog starts barking. I can see Cheeseburger's back starting to arch. I pull her towards me. 'I wish the dog wouldn't bark every time he sees my cat.'

Joey pats him on the head. 'He's a puppy. He just wants to play.'

The puppy might want to play, but the cat doesn't. I don't think the dog understands that Cheeseburger isn't

having an easy time with this *second pet* thing. 'So what are you guys doing?' I ask.

'Max asked me to help him name his dog,' says Joey.

I help myself to a slice of pizza and look in Max's direction. 'Can I help too?'

Max shoves pizza in his mouth. 'Aren't you supposed to be in your room?'

'I'm out.'

Max shoves in more pizza and shrugs.

'Naming a dog should be a family decision,' I tell Max.

'Naming a dog is a family decision,' says Dad. He and Mum walk into the kitchen and sit down at the table.

'Max invited Joey to help.' Dad scratches Max's dog behind his ears. 'We're all going to find a name for this dog by playing a game called the *Name Game*.'

'How do you play the *Name Game*?' I ask.

Dad takes a notepad and a pencil from the desk drawer in the kitchen. 'First, we're going to set a few rules. Then everyone brainstorms until we find a name we like.'

'What are the rules?' Max asks.

'The first rule should be that everybody has to like the name,' I say. 'Remember what Dad said, '*Naming a dog is a family decision.*''

Max frowns. 'The family can *help* name the dog, but the final decision is mine.'

I cross my arms. 'NOT FAIR!'

'IT IS FAIR!' says Max. 'I want a name I like. The first rule should be that the name has to do with baseball.'

'Baseball! I don't want a dog named Baseball.'

Max looks at me like I have a baseball for a brain. 'His name won't be Baseball. It will have something to do with baseball.'

'Why would you want to name a dog after something that has to do with baseball?' I ask Max.

Max shrugs. 'Why would you name a cat after a food?'

'Cheeseburger is named after my favourite food.' I hug Cheeseburger.

'It's a stupid name for a cat.'

'IS NOT!'

'IT IS!'

'THAT'S ENOUGH!' Dad puts his fingers in his mouth and whistles.

'Rule number one of the *Name Game*: the name has to relate to baseball. Rule number two: no fighting.' Dad looks at Max and me. 'Let's work together.'

'Fine.' Max says *fine* like working with me is only fine because Dad said he has to.

I came out of my room with a new

attitude. But I think Max needs to go to his room to change his. I'm trying to help and he's not acting like he cares if I do.

Dad pushes the pad and pen into the middle of the table. 'OK, the last thing we need is a secretary and then we're ready to play. Any volunteers?'

I grab the pad. 'I'll be the secretary.' I give Mum and Dad an *I'm-trying-to-get-along-with-Max* look, but I don't think Mum and Dad understand that getting along with Max isn't easy.

Dad snaps his fingers. 'How about Babe? Like Babe Ruth, the baseball player.'

If you ask me, it sounds like a baby, but I write Babe on the sheet of paper.

'What about Shortstop?' says Mum.

I've never heard of a dog named Shortstop. Still, as the official secretary, I add Shortstop to the list.

'How about Home Run?' says Joey. 'I think that's a great name for a dog.'

I write Home Run on the paper in front of me, but it sounds silly to me.

'They're all good names,' says Max. 'But none of them seem just right.'

I rub my forehead to help me think. 'How about Hot Dog?' I write the word Hot Dog in big letters across the top of the list. 'I think that name is just right.'

'How is the name Hot Dog just right?' asks Max.

I explain. 'Both pets will be named after foods. Since Cheeseburger and Hot Dog are sort of like brother and sister, it makes sense.'

Max scratches his head. I can't tell if he's thinking or if he has fleas. 'What does Hot Dog have to do with baseball?'

I feel as if I'm talking to an alien from

outer space who has never been to a baseball game. 'You eat hot dogs at the ballpark.'

Max reaches across the table and crosses Hot Dog off the list. 'I don't like it. It's weird to have two pets named after food.'

'Max should at least consider my suggestion,' I say to Mum and Dad.

Mum nods. 'Max, consider all the names.'

I add Hot Dog to the list again, but Max puts his head on the table. 'Finding a name is really hard,' he says.

'You'll know the right name when you hear it,' says Joey. He looks as if he feels sorry for Max, but I don't. I'm trying to help Max and he considered everybody's names but mine. Mum said this would be a family dog, but I think Max forgot that.

Max picks his head up. 'I've got it . . . Champ! Farmer Frank said this dog is a real champ. It's a perfect name because he's a *champ* and it has to do with baseball.'

'I like it,' says Dad.

'So do I,' says Mum.

'Me too,' says Joey.

Max holds his dog in the air. 'Champ, how do you like your name?'

Champ barks.

Dad pats him on the head. 'I think he loves it.'

Maybe Champ loves his new name, but I don't. 'Shouldn't we all get to help pick?' I ask.

Mum and Dad look at each other. Dad puts his arm across my shoulders.

'Sweet Potato, sometimes it takes a while to get used to a new name. Why don't you give it some time and I'm sure you'll see that Champ is a great name.'

I don't see what's so great about it. Mum and Dad let Max pick a name that I didn't even like. Dad said we would play the *Name Game,* but I think the only game Mum and Dad played was *Favourites,* and Max won. I push my pencil and papers into the middle of the table. I don't feel like being the secretary anymore.

Mum clears the pizza box from the table. 'Now that we've got the name out of the way, I think it's time to start training Champ.'

Joey rubs Champ's back. 'I'm pretty good at dog training. I've had a lot of practice with Murphy. Want me to help?'

Max grins. 'Can we start tomorrow?'

'OK,' says Joey. 'But everybody in your family should start too. When you're training a dog, it's best if everybody does the same thing.'

Joey looks at Mum, Dad and me. 'When I took Murphy to dog school, the trainer told me to bring Winnie, Dad and Grandpa. It really helped.'

'Sounds great,' says Dad. 'Just tell us when and where and we'll *all* be there.'

I get up and dump the rest of my pizza in the bin. Like it or not, dog school, here I come.

SATURDAY BLUES

My idea of a perfect Saturday morning is eating doughnuts on the couch with Cheeseburger and watching TV in my pyjamas. That's what I do every Saturday morning . . . except for today.

Today, Cheeseburger and I are standing in the front garden in a line with Mum and Dad and Max. Today we're students at the Wish Pond Road Dog School.

Joey blows a whistle. 'Let's work on sitting. When you want Champ to sit, look him in the eyes, point to the ground and say, *'Champ, sit.'* Then push his hindquarters down with your finger.'

Joey demonstrates *how-to-get-a-dog-to-sit* with his dog, Murphy. Then he blows his whistle again. 'Mallory, you're first.'

I look next door. Winnie is sitting on her front porch reading a magazine. She's lucky. She doesn't have to spend her Saturday morning at dog school.

Joey blows his whistle. I put Cheeseburger down on the ground. I look Champ firmly in the eyes. 'Champ, sit.'

Champ barks. But Champ doesn't sit.

'Mallory, push down his hindquarters. Try again.'

I point to the ground. 'Champ, sit!'

Champ wags his tail. Champ doesn't sit.

'Mallory, you have to push down his hindquarters,' says Joey.

I blow a piece of hair out of my eyes. 'I'm *not* pushing down hind anything. I don't think Champ is ready for sitting lessons.'

I point to Cheeseburger, who is sitting nicely by herself on the front lawn. 'I never taught Cheeseburger to sit. She just did. I don't know why we need to teach Champ. He'll work it out himself.'

'I bet I can get him to sit,' says Max.

I roll my eyes. 'Want to bet?'

Max flicks a piece of fuzz off his sweatshirt. 'Yeah. I'll bet you all the housework I'm meant to do this afternoon that I can get Champ to sit on the first try.'

'And what happens if he doesn't?' I ask.

'If Champ sits the first time I tell him to, you have to do all my housework. If he doesn't, I'll do yours.'

I think about my unmade bed and the stack of plates in the sink. 'It's a bet!'

Mum shakes her head. 'This is silly.'

'We're working together to train Champ,' says Dad. 'There's no need to bet.'

'I don't care if we bet,' says Max. 'It's up to Mallory.'

I like the idea of Max doing my housework. I shake his hand. 'It's Mallory vs Max in the *Who-Can-Get-Champ-to-Sit-First* Contest.'

'OK.' Joey blows his whistle. 'May the best man or woman win.'

I cross my toes. I hope the winner of this bet is a woman.

Max looks Champ in the eye. 'Champ, sit.' He talks in a low, steady voice. He points to the ground. Then he pushes his hindquarters down with his finger.

Champ stops wagging his tail. He looks down at the ground.

No Champ, don't do it! I try to send the message from my brain to his. It doesn't work though. Champ sits. Right next to Cheeseburger!

'Yes!' Max jumps in the air and makes a victory sign with his arms. 'I win! I win the bet.' He pets Champ on the back. 'Good boy,' he says to Champ.

Max high-fives Joey. 'Yes! I knew he could do it. Way to go, Champ!'

I look down at Champ sitting next to Cheeseburger. Usually, Cheeseburger gets nervous when Champ gets close to her, but today she doesn't. She's just sitting there like she's not sure how she feels about Champ.

Champ barks softly, but Cheeseburger doesn't move.

'The only reason Champ sat is because he wanted to be next to Cheeseburger. He wants to play with her!' I say.

'Sitting is sitting,' says Max. He pats me on the back. 'Don't forget to take out the bins after you sweep the garage.' Max laughs like a windup toy that won't stop.

'Max, that's enough.' Dad gives him a stern look.

Max clears his throat. 'Sorry. I'm just really happy that Champ learned to sit.'

Joey rubs Champ behind the ears. 'It took Murphy a whole week of dog school to learn to sit. Champ is a really clever dog.'

'Can we teach him some more tricks?' Max asks Joey.

'Of course! We can teach him to lie down and roll over.'

Mum puts her arm around Max. 'Soon you'll have a well-trained dog.' She smiles at Joey. 'You run an excellent dog school.'

'School!' Max looks at Mum. 'Do you think I can bring Champ to school?'

Mum nods her head. 'I don't see why not. I'm sure everyone at Fern Falls Elementary will love meeting Champ.'

'Awesome!' Max looks as if he just hit a home run.

Max might think taking Champ to school

is a grand-slam idea, but I don't. 'Mum, I never took Cheeseburger to school. I don't know why Max gets to take Champ.'

'Mallory, you never asked if you could take Cheeseburger to school,' Mum says.

'This will be great,' Max says to Joey. 'We can teach Champ some more tricks so he'll be ready to go to school really soon.'

Joey nods as if he thinks that's a great idea, but I don't. More tricks mean more dog school. I put my hands on my hips. 'Haven't we had enough dog school for one day?' I ask.

'You probably have,' says Max. 'You have work to do.'

'Dad!' I give him my *sweeping-the-garage-is-no-way-to-spend-my-Saturday* look. Dad puts his arm around me. 'Sweet Potato, a deal is a deal. You shook on it.'

I scoop up Cheeseburger and march off

towards the garage.

'Maybe we can teach Champ to shake hands. Everyone at school will love that,' I hear Joey say to Max.

'*Awesome!*' Max says to Joey.

I open the door to the garage and look inside. Everything looks dark and dusty. I hear Max and Joey laughing in the front garden. If you ask me, this isn't *awesome.* This is *terrible!*

I put Cheeseburger on top of a pile of boxes. She stretches and lies down as if she likes it in here as much as she likes being on my bed. Maybe she likes it in here, but I don't.

I find a broom and start sweeping.

Then, I start thinking.

Before Champ came along, I used to play with Joey on Saturdays. But now, he's busy with Max. I finish sweeping, then I pick up Cheeseburger. 'We're going to find someone else to play with,' I say out loud.

I march into the kitchen and dial my desk mate Pamela's phone number. I wait for the phone to ring. Pamela answers.

'Hi, Pamela. It's Mallory.' I use my cheery phone voice.

'Hi, Mallory. What are you doing?'

'I'm not doing anything and I wanted to see if you could come over and play.' I talk in my super cheery phone voice. I really want Pamela to come over.

'That sounds like fun,' says Pamela, 'but I can't. I have violin lessons.'

'Oh.' I guess I don't say *oh* in a cheery voice because Pamela asks me if something is the matter.

I tell her about my Saturday. I tell her about dog school and about sweeping the garage. I tell her it hasn't been such a great day for me.

'Hmmm,' says Pamela. 'Sounds to me like you've got Saturday Blues.'

'Saturday Blues?'

'I'll explain when I see you at school on Monday. Time for violin lessons.'

'See ya.' I try to say goodbye in a cheery voice, but when I hang up, I don't feel so cheery.

I look out of the window at Joey and Max playing with their dogs. They're outside having fun and I'm stuck inside with something that sounds like a disease.

I think about Saturday Blues. I don't need Pamela to explain what they are. I know I've got them.

A NEW TUNE

'Letter for Mallory McDonald.' Mum hands out the post as if she's a postman.

It's from Mary Ann. I grab the envelope from Mum and head to my room.

'Let's go,' says Max.

'Where are we going?' I ask. I just got home from school and the only place I want to go is to my room to read my letter.

'We're going to see Mr Alvarez the vet,' Mum picks up her handbag. 'Champ is getting a checkup before Max takes him to school tomorrow.'

For the past three weeks, *all* Max and Joey have been doing is training Champ so Max can take him to school.

They taught Champ to sit.

They taught Champ to roll over.

They even taught Champ to shake hands.

When I asked Max if I could help train Champ too, he told me that he and Joey are *The Dog Training Duo.*

He said they did NOT want to be *The Dog Training Trio.*

If you ask me, Max is acting as if he forgot he has a sister and Joey is acting like he forgot he's my friend. At least I have Mary Ann.

I slide into the backseat of Mum's car next to Max and Champ and open my letter from my best friend.

Dear Mallory,

Hi! Hi! Hi! I got your letter and showed
Mum the list of all the stuff you asked me to
get you. (I hope you don't mind that I showed
her your letter, but I needed her to take me
shopping because it was a lot of stuff to
carry myself.)

When Mum read your letter, she said we
weren't going shopping. She said I couldn't
send you the stuff you asked for. (Sometimes
mums can be REALLY mean!)

I told her that it was an E-MER-GEN-CY
and that you and Cheeseburger would
probably starve to death if I didn't send stuff
soon, soon, soon.

But Mum said she was sure you wouldn't
stay in your room forever. (Was she right?
Are you still there?)

And then she said you should change your
tune. Do you know what that means? (I had

no idea, so I asked Mum to explain.) She said it means you should get a new attitude, and she means about the dog.

She says you're lucky to have a cute, little puppy and that you should smile and have fun with it. She says that's what kids are supposed to do when they get a puppy.

OK. I have to go to hip-hop. Write back and tell me if you have a new tune yet.

Tra-la-la-la-la!

Love, Mary Ann

I crumple up Mary Ann's letter and shove it into my pocket. Nobody, not even my best friend, understands how hard it is to live with Max and Champ.

Mum pulls into the car park of Mr Alvarez's office and we take Champ inside. The receptionist tells us to have a seat in the waiting room.

'What do you think of my new puppy?' Max says to her.

'He's adorable.' She smiles at Max.

Max smiles back and pats Champ on the head, but I frown.

Max is the one who needs a new tune. Not me! The only song he ever sings is 'Everyone Pay Attention to Me and My Dog,' and I'm getting sick of that song.

'Champ McDonald.' A nurse in a white hat and uniform calls out Champ's name and leads us down the hall. We go into examining room number three. She tells Max to hold Champ on the examining table. 'The vet will be right with you.'

'The vet is here.' Mr Alvarez walks into the room and grins. 'How's Champ today?' Mr Alvarez looks happy to see Champ, but Champ doesn't look happy to see Mr

Alvarez. He tries to hide inside Max's sweatshirt.

Mr Alvarez rubs Champ's back.

'Mr Alvarez, I have a dog joke,' I say. 'What should a person do if they have a sick dog?'

'What's that, Mallory?' Mr Alvarez rubs the fur behind Champ's ears.

'Take him to the dogtor!'

Mr Alvarez smiles. 'I love good dog jokes, but taking a puppy to the vet is no laughing matter. Sometimes they get scared. They're like little babies.'

I never thought of Champ as a little baby before. I look at him next to Mr Alvarez. His nose is quivering and his legs are shaking. I remember when I was little, I used to be scared to go to the doctor. Sometimes, I still am.

'So what can I do for you today?'

Mr Alvarez asks Mum.

'I'm taking Champ to school tomorrow,' says Max. 'Mum said she wants to make sure everything is OK.'

'Good idea.' Mr Alvarez looks in Champ's ears. He does all the same stuff to Champ that my doctor does to me when I go for a checkup. He listens to his heart and lungs, checks inside his mouth and squeezes his tummy.

He looks at Max. 'There are some rules I want you to follow when you take Champ to school tomorrow. If you do, I think Champ will get an A+ on his first day of school.

'Rule 1: Hold on to Champ. He might get nervous around all those kids.

'Rule 2: Don't give him anything to eat or drink when you get to school.' Mr Alvarez smiles. 'You wouldn't want him to leave

any surprises in the classroom.

'Rule 3: Walk him before you take him into your classroom. I call that the *just-in-case* rule.' Mr Alvarez pats Max on the back. 'Can you handle it?'

Max nods. 'No problem.'

'You have to remember that puppies are a lot like people,' says Mr Alvarez. 'Sometimes they're scared to try new

things.'

Sometimes I'm scared to try new things
too. I remember how scared I felt on my
first day of school. I've never thought
about Champ as a person before. I think
about what Mary Ann said in her letter,
about changing my tune. Maybe I do need
a new tune when it comes to Champ.

We say good-bye to Mr Alvarez, and Max

carries Champ out to the car.

'Tomorrow is a big day for Champ,' Max says as Mum drives out of the car park.

It's a big day for Max too. Everybody in Max's class is going to meet Champ. I think about my new tune. Maybe now is a good time to start singing it. 'Max, do you think I could take Champ to my classroom too?'

Max looks as if I asked him to jump off the Empire State Building. 'NO WAY!'

'Please?' I ask in my *new-tune* voice. 'I would love for my class to meet Champ.'

I reach over and rub Champ's back. Max pulls Champ to his side of the back seat.

Mum looks in the rear-view mirror. 'Max, I think it would be nice for Mallory to take Champ to her classroom.' She gives Max an *I'm-hoping-you'll-change-your-mind-without-my-having-to-ask-again* look.

Max looks annoyed. 'Fine. Mallory can

take Champ to her class, but she has to
follow all of Mr Alvarez's rules.'

'No problem.' I can't believe Max said
yes. Maybe I'm not the only one changing
my tune. I can't wait to call Pamela and
tell her. 'I promise I'll follow all of Mr
Alvarez's rules,' I say, but Max doesn't
look convinced.

I raise my right hand like I've seen

people do in courtrooms on TV. 'I, Mallory McDonald, do solemnly swear to follow every single one of Mr Alvarez's rules.'

Max takes a deep breath. 'I'll be the judge of that,' he tells me.

SHOW AND SMELL

Rub-a-dub-dub, there's a dog in my tub!

Actually, it's Max's bathtub too. I never pictured a dog in there. 'What are you doing?' I ask Max.

He pours water over Champ's head. 'I want Champ to smell good when he goes to school today.'

I start to tell Max that dogs don't belong in the bath, but then I remember my new

tune. 'Want to use some of my Mango
Madness Shampoo? It smells yummy.'

'You don't think it'll be weird if Champ
smells like a mango?' says Max.

'Nope.' I squirt Mango Madness on
Champ's back and rub it around. Champ is
covered in white bubbles.

'He looks more like a sheep than a dog,'
says Max.

'You can tell everybody at school he's a
sheepdog.' I laugh at my joke.

Max looks serious. 'Dad is bringing
Champ to me after lunch. I'm showing him
to my class. Then I'm bringing him to you
to show to your class.'

Max rinses Champ off, then takes him
out of the bath. He starts drying him off
with a towel. 'You have to follow Mr
Alvarez's rules: hold on to him, don't give
him anything to eat or drink and walk him

before you take him into your classroom.'

I nod. 'Nothing will go wrong.'

Max fastens Champ's collar around his neck. 'Nothing will go wrong if you follow the rules.'

Mum comes into the bathroom and takes a picture of Max holding Champ. 'So you'll always remember Champ's first day of school,' she says to Max.

After breakfast, Max and I walk to school with Joey. 'So today's the big day,' Joey says to Max. 'Did Champ get a good night's sleep?'

Max nods. 'I hope Champ does a good job when he does his tricks.'

'I'm sure he will,' says Joey.

I clear my throat. 'Did Max tell you I get to take Champ to our class?'

Joey looks at Max as if that's something big that Max forgot to tell him. 'Do you know how to make him sit and shake paws and roll over?' Joey asks me.

I shake my head. 'I'm not going to do any tricks with him.'

'I can help you do some tricks if you want me to,' says Joey.

'No thanks.' I don't want Joey to be the one who shows Champ to my class. I want to be the one who does the showing.

We walk in the front gate of Fern Falls Elementary. 'See you after lunch,' Max says. Joey and I walk into our classroom.

'Good morning, class,' says Mrs Daily. 'Let's all take our seats and get started.'

My desk mate Pamela leans over to my side of the desk. 'Where's Champ?'

I start to tell Pamela he's coming after lunch, but Mrs Daily stops me. 'Mallory, why don't you tell the class about the

visitor you're bringing this afternoon for Show and Tell.' Everyone turns around to look at me.

'I'm bringing Champ.' I pause. I'm not sure how to say who Champ is to me. I don't feel like he's my dog and I don't want to say he's my brother's dog.

'Champ is a dog,' I tell the class.

Lots of kids start talking about their dogs. Pete tells the class that his dog just had puppies. Adam says he can imitate his dog and starts barking.

Mrs Daily taps her desk frog, Chester, which is what she does when she wants the class to be quiet. He croaks and the class stops talking. 'Let's work on maths and spelling,' says Mrs Daily. 'After lunch, you'll have a chance to share some stories about your furry friends.'

'I can't wait to meet Champ,' Pamela

whispers to me.

I can't wait to introduce Champ!

At lunch, the kids in my class want to know all about Champ. 'Does he sleep in your room?' Grace asks me.

'He sleeps in the utility room.' Joey answers Grace's question before I get a chance to. He says *'in the utility room'* like Champ sleeps in *his* utility room.

'How often do you feed him?' Zack wants to know.

'Twice a day.' Joey answers the question before I can even open my mouth. He says *'twice a day'* like he's the one who feeds Champ twice a day.

'Is it hard to train a puppy? I bet it is,' says April.

'Not at all,' says Joey. 'Champ is a fast learner. He's been really easy to train.'

Pamela picks up her rubbish and walks

over to the dustbin. She has a funny look on her face when she comes back. 'It seems like Joey knows a lot about Champ.'

I shrug. 'I suppose Joey does know a lot about Champ,' I tell Pamela. If you ask me, Joey is acting like he's a *know-it-all* and like I'm a *know-nothing.*

As Pamela and I walk back to our classroom after lunch, we see Max in the hall. He has Champ with him. 'Dad brought Champ early. I already showed him to my class.'

Max puts Champ in my arms. 'Take him to your class now, but don't forget Mr Alvarez's rules. Hold him. Don't give him anything to eat or drink. And walk him.' Max repeats the list of rules like I'm a two-year-old who can't remember anything.

'Don't worry,' I tell Max. 'I know how to take care of Champ.'

Outside my classroom, everyone crowds around for a better look.

'OOOOH! He's so cute,' says Arielle. 'Can I hold him?'

'Max told me the vet said no one is supposed to hold him,' Joey whispers.

Max and Joey are acting like I don't know the first thing about taking care of Champ. I think they are both forgetting that I am a longtime pet owner.

'I don't know why he'd be scared if one girl holds him,' I say to Joey. I hand Champ over to Arielle. I smile at Arielle. 'Isn't he cute?'

Arielle hugs Champ to her. 'He's adorable,' she says and passes him to Danielle. Danielle passes him on to Pete and Pete passes him on to Sammy.

Champ's nose starts quivering.

'He looks scared,' Joey says to me.

I look at Champ. This is my dog, not Joey's. 'He's not scared,' I say to Joey. 'He's excited to meet new people.'

Pete looks at Champ. 'He looks hungry.' Pete takes a piece of leftover turkey sandwich out of his lunch and feeds it to Champ.

'Mallory, Max told me the vet said he's not supposed to eat or drink anything at school,' Joey says to me.

I watch Champ chew on Pete's sandwich. I shrug my shoulders. 'He looks like he likes it,' I tell Joey.

Pete takes out his thermos, pours some milk into the top and holds it up to Champ's mouth. Champ slurps it up.

Joey looks at me as if I'm about to cross the road without looking both ways, I ignore his look. He's my friend, not my mother or a vet, and I don't see how a little milk to wash down a sandwich can hurt Champ.

Mrs Daily motions everyone back into the classroom.

'You have to walk Champ before you take him inside.' Joey stands in front of me with his arms crossed.

I don't remember anyone putting Joey in charge of making sure I follow the rules. I pretend like I'm at the wish pond and wish for some earplugs. I don't like listening to

Joey tell me what to do.

'My dog does not need to go for a walk just now.' I step around Joey and follow Mrs Daily inside.

'Mallory, why don't you introduce Champ,' she says when everyone is seated.

I walk to the front of the classroom holding Champ. 'This is Champ.' I hold him up and turn him from side to side so everybody can get a good view.

'Mallory, why don't you tell us a little bit about Champ,' Mrs Daily says.

I tell the class how we went to the farm to get Champ.

'Can he do any tricks?' Grace asks.

I think about all the training Max and Joey did. 'He can sit and roll over and shake paws,' I say.

'Make him sit,' says Zack.

Joey gives me a *do-you-want-some-help*

look. I ignore him. Champ is my dog too,
and I've seen Max and Joey do this dozens
of times.

I look Champ in the eye. 'Champ, sit.'

Champ wags his tail.

'Hey, Mallory . . . ' Joey tries to say
something, but I ignore him.

'Champ, sit!' I point to the ground.
Champ wags his tail even harder. He looks
as if he's about to sit.

Joey waves his arms at me from the back
of the class. But I pretend I can't see him.
I'm in charge of Champ. Not Joey.

'CHAMP, SIT!' I say it like I mean it. I
even push his hindquarters down to the
ground with my finger.

Champ sniffs the floor.

'MAL-LOR-Y!' Joey says my name syllable
by syllable, like he's talking to a baby. I
look at him and he gives me a *you-need-my-*

help look, but I don't.

I watch while Champ lowers his tail to the ground. I can't believe it! Champ is finally going to sit for me.

'See,' I say to the class. 'Champ is excellent at doing tricks.' I give Joey an *I-finally-got-it-right* look.

But Joey is looking at me like something is very wrong. I look down at Champ.

'Look what Champ is doing!' Danielle screams.

There's a yellow puddle under Champ and it's spreading out all over the floor. There's a little brown pile too.

'This isn't Show and Tell.' Arielle holds her nose. 'This is Show and Smell!'

Laughter fills the classroom.

Mrs Daily bangs on Chester's head. 'Quiet class, that's enough.' She hands me a roll of paper towels. 'Why don't you wipe that up,' she says gently.

I take the paper towels from her. But there's more giggling as I bend down to clean up Champ's mess.

I don't look up, but I feel like Joey is giving me a *none-of-this-would-have-happened-if-you-had-just-listened-to-me-and-followed-the-rules* look.

I know how Cinderella must have felt when she didn't follow the rules and her coach turned into a pumpkin.

She was lucky. She had a fairy godmother to make it better. All I have is a handful of paper towels.

WINNERS AND LOSERS

'THIS IS YOUR FAULT!' Max throws his backpack on the kitchen floor.

'MY FAULT?' I throw my backpack on the floor on top of his.

'YOUR FAULT!' screams Max. His face is as red as a bowl of tomato soup. 'Joey said you didn't follow any of Mr Alvarez's rules. If you had, none of this would have happened!'

Joey is a telltale. I can't believe he told Max. I also can't believe Max thinks this is my fault. 'I'm not the one who pooed and peed on the floor at school!' I point to Champ. 'If you want to be angry, be angry at that stupid dog, not at me.'

'How can you call him a stupid dog?' Max looks at me as if I'm the one who's missing brain cells. 'Do you know how embarrassed he must have been?'

'How embarrassed *he* must have been? Champ is a dog! How do you think I felt? Today was the most embarrassing day of my life. I'll never be able to go back to school.'

'Good,' says Max. 'I hope you don't.'

Dad puts his fingers between his teeth and whistles. 'MAX, MALLORY, THAT'S ENOUGH!' He points to the living room. 'Time for a family talk.'

Max and I follow Mum and Dad into the living room and sit on the couch – Max on one end, Cheeseburger and me on the other.

Dad clears his throat. I feel as if Max and I are about to get a *you-better-hear-every-word-I-have-to-say-and-change-your-behaviour-immediately* talk, and I'm right.

Dad crosses his arms across his chest. 'I'm tired of the fighting and arguing that

goes on around here. Ever since we decided to get a dog, all you two have done is fight.'

Max raises his hand. 'Can I say something?'

'Not yet.' Dad shakes his head. 'I want you to hear what I have to say. A family doesn't fight. A family works together, like a team. Getting a dog is about working together to train the dog and making it a part of our team.'

Dad is wrong. Maybe some families work together like a team, but not ours. In this family, there are two teams, mine and Max's, and whenever there are two teams, one team wins and one team loses. Lately, I am ALWAYS on the losing side.

Max raises his hand again. 'Now may I say something?'

Dad looks annoyed. 'What is it, Max?'

'Ever since we got Champ, Mallory hasn't done one thing to take care of him. I'm the one who does everything. So isn't Champ my dog?'

Dad looks at me. 'Mallory found Cheeseburger. She has always taken care of her, but Cheeseburger is part of this family.' Dad looks at Max. 'We got Champ because you wanted a dog, but Champ is a member of this family too.'

Max is quiet.

I'm not though. 'Max can have Champ. He doesn't even like me. If he did, he wouldn't have pooed on the floor and embarrassed me in front of my whole class.'

'Mallory,' says Mum. 'Champ going to the toilet on the floor doesn't have anything to do with him liking or not liking you. You were supposed to follow a few rules and you didn't do that.'

Dad crosses his arms. 'Mallory, you should have taken better care of Champ. You and Max need to learn to treat each other with kindness and respect. I want you both to go to your rooms and give some serious thought to your roles in this family.'

I pick up Cheeseburger. My room is the ONLY place I want to be right now.

Max stands up and calls Champ. 'Champ, here boy.'

But Champ doesn't come.

Max calls his name louder. 'Champ!'

Champ still doesn't come.

'Has anyone seen Champ?' Max walks into the kitchen. 'Champ! Here boy!'

Mum and Dad and I follow Max into the kitchen. Champ isn't there and the kitchen door is open.

'Mallory! You left the back door open!' Max calls Champ's name out the back door, but Champ doesn't come.

I think about what happened when we got home from school. Max yelled at me. I yelled at him. Max threw his backpack on the floor. I threw mine on top of his.

Then . . . *did* I close the door?

I put Cheeseburger down on the kitchen floor. I run to the back door and call Champ's name too. 'CHAMP!'

We all go outside to look for him.

'CHAMP!' Dad calls his name.

'CHAMP!' Mum calls his name.

'MALLORY!' Max says my name like the sound of it makes him feel sick. 'Champ is gone and it's all your fault!'

DOG GONE!

'We'll find him,' says Dad.

'Let's split up,' says Mum. 'Max, go next door and get Joey. Mallory, you go down to the wish pond. Dad and I will check inside.'

We split up and start the hunt.

I run to the wish pond.

I think about what Max said. *Champ is gone and it's all your fault.*

I feel as if it is my fault. I was so cross with Champ today at school, I didn't think I'd ever be un-cross. Now all I want to do is find him.

When I get to the wish pond, I look under rocks and behind trees. I call Champ's name. I remember what Mr Alvarez said: *Puppies are a lot like little babies.* I would have been really scared if I'd got lost when I was a baby.

'Champ!' I say again. 'Please, please, please come out.' But he doesn't.

I pick up a stone on the side of the wish pond, close my eyes and make a wish. *I wish we'll find Champ.* I squeeze the stone in my hand and throw it in.

Even though he's only been gone for a little while, I miss him. If we ever find him, I'm going to show him that everybody in our family loves him, including me.

Then I pick up another stone. *I wish Max and I could get along and not fight.*

I know he thinks it's my fault that Champ
is missing. I want to find a way to make it
up to Max. I throw my stone in the water.

'MALLORY!'

I hear Joey call my name.

I see him running down the road towards
the wish pond. When he gets to me, he's
out of breath. 'Did you find him?'

I shake my head *no*. I wish I had a
different answer.

'No one else has seen him either,' says

Joey. He's breathing hard. 'Let's go from house to house. Maybe one of the neighbours has seen him.'

I follow Joey. I still can't believe he told Max that what happened today was my fault. I don't want to go with him, but I do want to find Champ.

Joey and I walk to the first house on our road and ring the doorbell. Mrs Black answers. 'I'm sorry,' she says when we explain what's going on. 'I haven't seen Champ.' She looks at us like there's nothing worse than a missing puppy.

'Thanks.' I try to smile at Mrs Black, but it's hard to be happy when your brother's dog is gone and it's your fault.

Joey and I knock on more doors. The Martins'. The Fines'. The Walkers'. No one has seen Champ. I look up at the sky. It's starting to get dark. I hope we find Champ before night-time.

Joey and I walk up to the Harts' house and ring the bell. No one answers. 'I wonder if Mrs Hart is home,' says Joey.

'I don't know.' When I talk, my voice sounds funny, like it's not my own.

Joey looks at me. 'Mallory, are you cross about something?'

I can't even believe Joey has to ask me that. 'Why did you tell Max that the accident in the classroom was my fault?'

Joey pushes the doorbell again. 'I tried to tell you to follow Mr Alvarez's rules, but you wouldn't listen.'

I take a deep breath. 'Today at school, you were acting like Champ was your dog. It made me mad. I wanted to prove that I know how to take care of Champ, without everybody telling me what to do. I wanted to feel like he was my dog too.'

Joey looks at me. 'I'm sorry if I was acting like Champ was mine.'

'Ever since Max got Champ, you've practically ignored me,' I tell Joey. 'You used to not even like Max and all of a sudden, you're his best friend.'

'Mallory, I'm sorry you think I've been ignoring you. I wasn't trying to. I was just helping Max take care of Champ. Just because I spend time with Max doesn't mean you and I aren't friends.'

'MALLORY! JOEY!' Dad calls our names and motions for us to come back.

'Maybe they found him!' I tell Joey. We run to my house. Mum, Dad, Max, Winnie and Mr Winston are in my front garden.

'Did you find him?' I ask. I'm out of breath from running.

'NO! And it's almost night-time,' says Max. He looks upset.

'The only thing worse than a D-O-G is a L-O-S-T D-O-G,' says Winnie. She looks at me like it's my fault that Champ is missing.

I look down at the ground. I wish there was something else I could do.

'Let's think about this,' says Mum. 'We've checked the house, the wish pond, the back garden.'

'We searched our house too,' says Mr Winston.

'He can't have gone too far,' says Dad.

'Did anybody check the garage?' I ask.

Max shakes his head. 'I didn't check in the garage. I was looking outside.'

'We didn't check the garage,' says Mum. 'We were in the house.'

I can't believe no one checked the garage! 'Maybe Champ went into the garage,' I say. 'Cheeseburger loves it in there.'

We all run to see if Champ is in the garage. Mum flips on the light. 'Champ!' Max calls his name. We wait to hear a woof-woof, but we don't.

'Champ!' Max calls his name again.

We don't hear a woof-woof, but we do hear a soft meow.

'That must be Cheeseburger,' says Mum.

'Cheeseburger.' I call her name and she meows again...a little louder this time.

'It's coming from over there.' Joey points to the corner of the garage.

I step over some boxes and look in the corner.

Cheeseburger is curled up on a pile of old blankets. 'Cheeseburger is here,' I tell everybody, 'and so is Champ!' Champ is curled up asleep next to Cheeseburger.

'I wonder how Champ got in the garage,' says Max.

'I must have left the door open the other day when I was sweeping,' I say.

I pick up Champ, give him a hug and hand him to Max.

Then I pick up Cheeseburger and hug her too. 'Cheeseburger must have found Champ and kept him safe.'

I've never been so happy to see a cat . . . or a dog.

TEAMMATES

'Who wants a brownie?' asks Mum. 'This is a celebration!'

I help Mum pass around a plate of brownies to Max, Joey, Winnie and Mr Winston. Dad fills glasses of milk.

Even though I've already had a hamburger and a hot dog, I take two brownies. I don't know why, but looking for a lost dog made me hungry.

I take a bite of my brownie. Then I pour some of my milk into Cheeseburger's bowl.

'Good kitty,' I rub her back. 'I'm proud of you for finding Champ.' I pat Champ on the head. 'I'm proud of you too. You found a nice spot and went to sleep.'

Max takes another brownie. 'He's a clever dog.'

'He is clever,' I tell Max, 'but he needs a little more work in the *things-we-do-inside* and *things-we-do-outside* departments.'

Winnie pushes her plate away. 'I heard about Show and Smell. That's soooooo gross!' She holds her nose.

Joey looks at Winnie like she has no clue what she's talking about. 'It wasn't that big a deal.' Then he smiles at me like it *really* wasn't a big deal.

I smile at Joey. Even though he's been spending a lot more time with Max than with me lately, I know he's trying to make me feel better about what happened.

I rub Champ's back and he rubs up against my leg. 'Hey, I think he likes me.'

'Of course he likes you,' says Mum. 'All you have to do is show him that you care about him.' Mum winks at me. 'Puppies are a lot like little babies.'

I smile at Mum. 'I've heard that before.'

When everyone finishes their brownies, the Winstons say goodbye. 'It's a school day tomorrow,' says Mr Winston.

After they leave, I start to go to my room to get ready for bed, but Dad stops me. 'Mum and I would like to see you and Max in the living room.'

I can't believe it . . . another family talk! I give Max a *what-did-we-do-this-time* look, but he looks as confused as I am. Max and I sit down on the sofa.

'I'm proud of the two of you,' says Dad. 'We had a bad situation this afternoon and our whole family worked together to solve it.' Dad nods as if he approves of our behaviour. 'I'd like to see our family working as a team more often.'

Mum smiles too. 'I like thinking of us as teammates,' she says.

'Mum, Dad,' I say. 'I don't feel like much of a teammate. If I hadn't left the back door open, Champ wouldn't have got lost.' I look down at a dirt spot on my jeans. 'Max, I'm really sorry.'

'I'm sorry too,' mumbles Max. 'I shouldn't have said it was all your fault. If I had been watching Champ, he never would have run away.'

Mum and Dad smile at each other. 'Fortunately,' says Dad. 'Champ didn't run far. He and Cheeseburger found a safe place together.'

'Speaking of together,' says Mum, 'no

one move.' She gets her camera. 'I want a picture of both of you with your pets.'

Max and I put Champ and Cheeseburger on our laps.

'Everybody smile and say, *'Getting along is a great idea.'*'

Max and I look at each other and roll our eyes. Sometimes Mum is such a mum. But I smile when she takes the picture and think about what she said. Getting along is a great idea. It's just not always easy to do.

I go into my room and put on my pyjamas. As I get into bed, I can't help thinking about what Dad said about working together as a team. Something about it still bothers me.

When Mum and Dad tuck me in, I tell them what's on my mind.

'Dad, you know what you said about teammates? Well, ever since we got

Champ, I feel like you and Mum have been paying a lot more attention to Max's team than to mine.'

Mum and Dad look at each other. 'Mallory, you and Max are both important to us,' says Dad. 'We try to give both of you lots of attention. Sometimes you might get a little more and sometimes Max might get a little more.'

I nod as if that makes sense to me, but I must l look confused.

'Mallory, do you remember when you found Cheeseburger?' Mum asks me.

I nod.

'Do you remember how we took her to the vet and went to the pet shop to buy her food and a bed?'

'Of course,' I say. 'I remember all of that.'

'We spent a lot of time helping you take care of Cheeseburger when we got her, just like we spent a lot of time helping Max take care of Champ when he got him.'

Dad puts his arm around me. 'Sweet Potato, do you understand what Mum and I are trying to say to you?'

'I've got it,' I say.

'Good,' Dad says. 'I'm glad what we've said makes sense.'

'I get what you're saying, but what I've got is an idea – a really, really, really great idea. Mum, may I have a copy of the picture you took of Max and Champ and me and Cheeseburger tonight?'

Mum nods her head, but she looks confused, so I explain.

'I'm going to make a Champ scrapbook for Max, just like my Cheeseburger scrapbook. Do you think Max will like it?'

'I think he'll love it,' says Mum.

She and Dad kiss me. 'Good night,' says Dad. 'It's been a long day.'

'I don't think I'll ever forget today,' I tell my parents. 'It didn't begin too well, but at least it had a happy ending.'

Everyone smiles . . . even me.

FAMILY FUN DAY

I started a new club.

It's called SABGD. That's short for
Sisters AND Brothers Getting Dogs. This
morning we're doing our first official club
activity.

I bang on Max's door. 'Wake up!' I
shout. 'It's time.'

I don't hear a sound from Max's room.
I bang again and then I open his door.
'WAKE UP!' I use Mum's *get-up-now-or-
you're-going-to-be-late* voice.

Max opens one eye. 'Is it a school day?'

Max must be the only brother on the planet who can't tell the difference between a school day and a day when our family is going to do something fun together.

'It's Family Fun Day. Remember?' I pull the covers off Max. 'Mum, Dad, Champ

and Cheeseburger are in the kitchen. We're waiting for you.'

Max doesn't move. I wait for him to say something Max-like, like *count me out*. But he surprises me.

'Give me five minutes,' Max says. 'I'll be right there.'

'Great! I'll start setting up.' I skip down the hall to the kitchen. If you ask me, Family Fun Day is going to be a lot of fun.

'Good morning!' I smile at Mum and Dad and take a mixing bowl out of the cabinet.

'Nice to see you looking so cheerful,' says Mum.

I start getting out the ingredients we'll need. Flour. Eggs. Salt. Powdered milk. Butter. 'I hope Champ likes these,' I say to Mum and Dad.

They smile at each other. 'Champ's a clever dog,' says Mum. 'I'm sure he'll be able to tell the difference between shop-bought and home-made.'

'Do you think Cheeseburger might like them too?' I ask.

Mum laughs. 'I suppose we could let her taste them.'

Max looks confused as he walks into the kitchen. 'Are we making dog biscuits or cat biscuits?'

'Dog biscuits.' I pass out copies of the home-made dog biscuit recipe that Pamela helped me find on the Internet. 'I think cats can eat them too.' I read off the list of ingredients in the recipe. 'Who knows, some people might even like them.'

Max makes a face. 'I'll stick with doughnuts.' He picks a chocolate one out of the box on the worktop.

I mix butter, water, powdered milk, salt and an egg in the bowl. It looks like slime.

'Want some help?' Mum takes the spoon from me and starts stirring.

I add flour. The slime is getting thick and sticky.

'Hey!' says Max. 'I want to help too. It's Family Fun Day. Remember?' He sticks his hands in the mixing bowl and starts forming the sticky stuff into a ball.

I dump flour and wheatgerm on the counter. 'The recipe says we have to roll the dough out and cut it into little bones.'

Max rolls. I cut. Dad greases a baking tray. Mum puts the treats in the oven. I look at my watch. 'Fifty minutes and we'll have home-made dog biscuits.'

Max takes another doughnut. 'In fifty minutes, *Champ* will have home-made dog biscuits. I already told you I'll help make them, but I'm not eating them.'

I think about the ingredients in dog

biscuits. Flour. Eggs. Milk. Butter. Even though I'd rather eat doughnuts than dog biscuits, someone should taste them to make sure they're OK for Champ.

I raise my hand. 'I volunteer to be the official dog biscuit taster.'

Mum and Dad smile at each other. 'Mallory, that's a nice offer,' says Dad. 'But let's leave the dog biscuit eating to Champ.'

'You guys go and tidy your rooms,' says Mum. 'When the dog treats are ready, we can keep enjoying Family Fun Day.'

'The cinema and miniature golf,' I say.

'Pizza and ice cream too,' says Max.

'Yes to all of the above. Now, off you go,' says Mum.

Max and I go into our rooms. I make my bed and then I sit down at my desk. I have a letter to write. I take out a sheet of paper and begin.

Dear Mary Ann,
I have three IMPORTANT THINGS to tell you:
IMPORTANT THING I: Champ got lost!
It was partly (not completely) my fault, but I felt completely (not partly) awful! We looked everywhere and couldn't find him. But guess who finally found Champ?
Cheeseburger! Cheeseburger found Champ and kept him safe.
I was so proud of Cheeseburger and not just for saving Champ. I thought she would have a really hard time having a new pet in our house, but she has handled it like a true champ. (Champ...champ, get the joke?) She loves that dog.

IMPORTANT THING 2:
I love Champ!
Even though
Champ is
sort of
max's dog,
I love him
too. When
max first got him, I
didn't think I would
ever like having him
in our family. But
when Champ was lost, I was really sad.
You were right. Champ is sweet and
cute and fun to play with.

IMPORTANT THING 3: I love max!
JUST KIDDING! THIS IS A JOKE!
Here's the truth: I don't hate max.
We're actually getting along. You're
probably wondering how that's possible.

I'll tell you. While Champ was missing, our whole family worked together to find him, and once we found him, Dad said how nice it was to see Max and me working together. He said he'd like to see us do it more often.

Max and I told Dad we didn't know how often we could actually do it, but we were sure we could do it for a day.

So today, we're having something called Family Fun Day. (Max said the name was totally stupid. When I asked if he had any suggestions, he said coming up with a good name is really hard to do and that we could keep it.)

So here's what we're doing on Family Fun Day: This morning, we made home-made dog biscuits. When the dog biscuits are finished cooking, we're going to play crazy golf and then we're going for pizza, and then to the cinema.

Mum and Dad said Max and I could do anything we wanted, but that we both had to agree. Then they made us promise we'd spend the whole day getting along.

I was going to write to you after tonight, but I was scared I'd be too tired. (Getting along with Max for a whole day will be exhausting!)

G2G (Got to go!)

The scent of freshly baked dog biscuits fills the air!

Big, huge hugs and kisses!
Mallory

PS You'll be happy to know I'm singing a new tune! It's called 'Mallory McDonald Has a New Pal.' (It sounds like 'Old McDonald Had a Farm.')

Here's how it goes:

mallory mcDonald has a new pal.
Woof! Woof! Woof! Woof! Woof!
At first, she didn't like him,
    but she does now.
Woof! Woof! Woof! Woof! Woof!
With a woof, woof here.
And a woof, woof there.
Here a woof. There a woof.

Everywhere a woof, woof.
Mallory McDonald has a new pal.
Woof! Woof! Woof! Woof! Woof!

A RECIPE FROM MALLORY

(In case you want to try this at home!)

HOME-MADE DOG BISCUITS

Here's what you'll need:

80 g butter or margarine

180 ml hot water (not too hot!)

175 ml powdered milk

1/8 teaspoon salt (not too much!)

1 egg (beaten)

300 g wholemeal flour

30 g wheatgerm (sounds gross, but dogs like it!)

Here's what you do:

Get out a big bowl. Put butter or margarine in the bowl and pour hot water over it. Stir in powdered milk, salt and egg. Add the flour, 50 g at a time. Form the dough into a ball with your hands. Put a little flour and wheatgerm on the worktop. Put the dough on top of it and roll it out with a rolling pin (or you can use your fingers) until it is two centimetres thick. Now (this is the fun part), cut the dough into bone shapes and place on a lightly greased baking tray. Bake these treats at 160°C for 50 minutes. Let them cool and they will dry out and harden. You can store them in a plastic bag in the refrigerator.

Making home-made dog biscuits is a little messy but dogs really, really, really like these treats.

Oh yeah and don't forget to check with your vet before you give these to your dog. You know how vets are – they have lots and lots and lots of rules!

CHAMP'S SCRAPBOOK

I thought you might like a sneak peep at
the scrapbook I'm making for Max.

Here's a
picture of the
day Max got
Champ from
Farmer Frank.

Here's a
picture of the
day Max took
Champ to
school.

Here's a picture of Max and Champ and Cheeseburger and me.

Mum said I should call this last picture the *Teammates* photo.

I told Mum I'm not naming any of the photos, but I am leaving lots of room for more. The thing is, I want this scrapbook to be really, really, really good. I don't want Champ to think, *'This is nice, but Mallory made a nicer one for Cheeseburger.'*

You know how it is when there are two pets in one family. Someone always feels like the other guy is more important. I hope Max and Champ like their scrapbook!

First published in the United Kingdom in 2009 by
Lerner Books,
Dalton House,
60 Windsor Avenue,
London SW19 2RR

Website address: www.lernerbooks.co.uk

This edition was updated and edited for UK publication by Discovery Books Ltd.,
First Floor, 2 College Street, Ludlow, Shropshire SY8 1AN

British Library Cataloguing in Publication Data

Friedman, Laurie B., 1964–
Mallory vs Max. – (Mallory)
1. Sibling rivalry – Juvenile fiction 2. Pets – Juvenile
fiction 3. Children's stories
1. Title
813.6[J]

ISBN-13: 978 0 7613 4288 5

First Published in the United States of America in 2005
Printed in Singapore